DATE DUE

FEB 0 6 1995			MAR 1 5 2011
MAR 1 4 1995	JUL 1 3 2000		FEB 2 8 2012
NOV 2 8 1997			DEC 2 6 2012
MAR 3 1 1998	AUG 1 3 2001		FEB 1 6 2013
JUN 3 1998	OCT 1 4 2005		
OCT 0 3 1998			AUG 0 5 2013
FEB 2 4 1999	DEC 1 0 2003		OCT 1 5 2013
	JUN 1 5 2004		JAN 2 1 2015
AUG 1 6 1999	JUN 2 5 2005		
SEP 1 5 1999	AUG 0 3 2005		MAY 4 2015
SEP 2 1 2000	JAN 0 5 2009		
NOV 1 6 2011			

JOJI AND THE DRAGON

BY BETTY JEAN LIFTON

Illustrated by

EIICHI MITSUI

E. Mitsui

LINNET BOOKS • HAMDEN, CONNECTICUT • 1989

To Bob, my scarer of dragons.

Published 1989 as a Linnet Book, an imprint of
The Shoe String Press, Inc., Hamden, Connecticut 06514.
First published 1957 by William Morrow & Company.

The paper used in this publication meets the
minimum requirements of American National Standard
for Information Sciences-Permanence of Paper for
Printed Library Materials, ANSI Z39.48—1984. ∞

Manufactured in the United States of America

Library of Congress Cataloging-in-Publication Data

Lifton, Betty Jean.
  Joji and the dragon / by Betty Jean Lifton; illustrated
by Eiichi Mitsui.
      p.   cm.
  Reprint. Originally published: New York : Morrow,
1957.
  Summary: With the help of his friends, a kind straw
scarecrow is able to prove he is scarier than Toho the
Terrible.
  ISBN 0-208-02245-7 (alk. paper)
  [1. Fairy tales.   2. Scarecrows—Fiction.
3. Crows—Fiction.   4. Japan—Fiction.]   I. Mitsui,
Eiichi, 1920–   ill.   II. Title.   88-8434
PZ8.L6225Jm   1989   CIP
[E]—dc19   AC

Once upon a time,
in a rice paddy in Japan,
there lived a straw scarecrow
named Joji.

Joji was a wonderful scarecrow
except for two things—
he didn't scare anyone,
and his best friends were crows.

But Joji never forgot
to guard the young rice plants.

He politely asked the crows
not to eat his rice.
And when they asked why,
he explained there was not enough rice
in all Japan
for both birds and people.

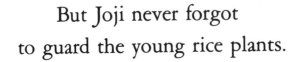

And because they loved Joji,
the crows promised
to leave the rice alone,
and to eat worms
for the rest of their lives.

However,
the farmer did not trust Joji
or the crows.
He was sure that the crows
were eating his rice.

So one day
the farmer decided to get a new scarecrow.
He put an ad on the village board
which read:

Wanted!
Some Spooky Person
To Scare Crows.
Straw Men Need Not Apply.

That night
a tremendous dragon knocked on the door
of the little farmhouse.
"I am Toho the Terrible,"
he said, bowing low.
"I would like the job
of scaring your crows."

"Come in,"
said the farmer,
"and have a cup of tea."

Toho the Terrible
     squeezed his huge body
          through the tiny doorway.

Surely he was a ferocious dragon!
     Savage smoke climbed cruelly over his head!
     His green slimy body slithered!
     His sharp red tongue spat fire!

"Have you had much experience
    scaring people?"
        asked the farmer,
           who was secretly very scared
           just looking at him.

"It is my lifework!"
    said the dragon,
    puffing on his flaming pipe.
"In the past five hundred years
    I have scared
        mighty emperors,
           handsome knights,
               beautiful princesses,
              good fairies,
                river elves. . . . "

"And crows?"

asked the farmer.

"Wa Ha Ha!"

      roared the dragon.

"Not only *Crows*—

      but *Scarecrows,* too!"

The farmer was so impressed
        by Toho the Terrible
that he bowed very low.
        "You're hired!"
           he said.
"Sleep here tonight
        and start work tomorrow."

Then he laid a Japanese bed on the floor
      of the guest room
        just for Toho,
          and tiptoed out.

Meanwhile,
a crow had been listening in the garden.
Frantically
he flew to Joji,
crash-landing on his head.

"The farmer has hired a dragon
to take your place!"
he cawed.

"A dragon! A dragon!"
      cawed all the crows.

"A dragon!"
        gasped Joji,
             feeling so weak
             he would have crumbled to the ground
             if a pole had not been holding him up.

    "What shall we do!"
    "What shall we do!"
             they all cried.

But no one could think of anything to do.

The next morning,
          bright and early,
     the farmer marched into the rice paddy
          and, without a word,
               dragged Joji away
               and tossed him into the barn.

Then Toho the Terrible
    brought a soft cushion
        from the house,
    and took his seat
        in Joji's old spot.

Alas, poor Joji!
He lay in a broken heap
        with a broken heart
    in the corner of the barn.

And every day
the dragon would pull some straw
        out of Joji's body
to fill his pipe,
            so that Joji got weaker and weaker,
            while the dragon got stronger and stronger.

                    Finally,
            when Joji was nothing more
                    than a few pieces of straw,
                    he called the crows into the barn
                        for his last words.

"Farewell, feathered friends,"
    he whispered weakly.
"Remember to be good Japanese crows
    and eat only worms when I am gone."

        At this
    the crows began to cry so hard and so long,
    their wet black coats shone in the darkness
        as brightly as their eyes.

"Do not be sad,"
    said Joji,
"for I would rather be here
    loved by you,
than mighty in the field
    scaring you away."

        And then Joji became so tired,
        he could not say another word.

Early the next morning
    before anyone was awake,
  the crows held a meeting
        in the rice paddy
      to decide what they could do
        to save Joji's life.

When the meeting was over,
  they slipped into the barn,
    picked Joji up,
  and carried his limp form through the sky.

They took him to a nearby haystack
   and stuffed his body with hay
until he was well and strong again.

"Oh, why did you save me?"
        sighed Joji miserably.
"What good is a scarecrow
        who doesn't like to scare crows,
        and doesn't know how to scare dragons?"

"Perhaps you will scare a dragon tonight,"
        cawed the crows.

"But how?"

asked Joji.

"You'll see,"

cawed the crows.

"You'll see."

Then the crows flew off toward the farmyard.
They looked like a black streak in the morning sky.

A few hours later
Toho the Terrible stopped in at the barn
to fill his pipe with Joji's straw.
But there was no Joji.

"Where is Joji?"
he roared.

"Joji flew away,"
said the largest, blackest crow,
sitting at a safe distance
on the rafter.

"Flew away?"
        roared Toho.
"Scarecrows can't fly."

"Joji can fly,"
        cawed the crow calmly.

"Wa Ha Ha,"
    laughed the dragon,
        spitting fire.
"Not even the ghost of that silly scarecrow
            could fly!"

"You'll see,"
        cawed the crow.
"You'll see."

That night,
at the stroke of midnight,
a few crows
flew to the farmer's window
and made so much noise
the old man woke with fright
and ran to get the dragon.

Toho the Terrible
    woke with a deep moan
        and roared out of the house so fast
        that everything shook
        as if there were an earthquake.

The one thing that made Toho fighting mad,
    was to have his sleep disturbed
        in the middle of the night.

Dark fumes flew from Toho's throat!
Fiery flames flared from his fangs!
   The very stars in heaven
      hid from sight,
         as this terrible dragon
            howled and growled,
               stoomphed and cloomphed
                  through the rice paddies
                   until . . .

there in the black night
he saw a pale, ghostly form
flying
through the sky.

"Joji's ghost!"
he cried.
"It's Joji's ghost!"

And then Toho turned on his tail,
and without stopping to pack his bag,
fled yowling down the road!

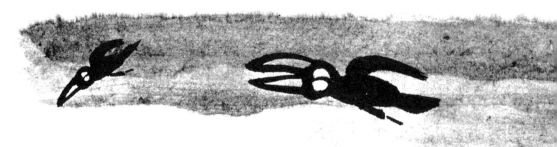

When the dragon was gone,
    the crows,
        who had been carrying Joji through the air,
          placed him gently on the ground
            in his old spot
              and flew about him, cawing:

                "Joji scared the dragon!"
                "Joji scared the dragon!"

while Joji,
    who was still dizzy from his flight,
        could only smile and say,
          "How lucky I am to have friends
             as swift as the wind,
             and as black as the night."

The farmer,

who had seen everything,

now bowed low to Joji

and begged him to keep his job

as scarecrow

for the rest of his life.

He even begged the crows

to stay on the farm

as his special guests.

And so
      Joji went back to his old spot
            in the rice paddies,
    and the crows went back
           to eating worms.

      But every night
when the farmhouse was asleep,
      the crows would gather around Joji
           to hear him tell again
about the time he scared the dragon.

      And
instead of calling him
           Joji the scarecrow,
they called him
           Joji the dragon-scarer,
           ever after.